TOBY'S
TIGHTROPE

buzz books

One day Percy arrived at the quarry to collect some stone for his trucks. Snow and frost lay everywhere. There was not a sound to be heard. Percy ventured further.

HENRY

JAMES

PERCY

He found Mavis, the new diesel engine, resting in the shelter of some rocks.

"Cheer up Mavis," he whistled.

Mavis was still remembering the trouble she'd had with trucks.

"Manager says I don't listen to advice. He says I've no business jauntering down Toby's line. Toby's a fusspot."

"Toby has forgotten more about trucks than you will ever know," replied Percy. "You must put the trucks where he wants them, then you'll be a Really Useful Engine. Now, if you'll excuse me, I have to take these stones to the harbour."

Mavis liked Percy but she still wouldn't listen to his advice.

"Why shouldn't I go on Toby's line?"

The siding arrangements were awkward.
To put the trucks where Toby wanted them
Mavis had to make several journeys.
She started making a plan.

"If we used the teeniest bit of Toby's line, we would save all this bother."

Her driver, suspecting nothing, allowed them to go as far as the first level crossing.

A few days later, the weather changed.
As the snow melted, the quarry grew
busy again.

Some trains were so long that Mavis had to go beyond the level crossing.

Now for her plan. She would go further down the line without it seeming her fault.

"Can you keep a secret?" she asked the trucks.

"Yes, yes, yes," they chattered.

"Will you bump me at the level crossing and tell no-one I asked you?"

The trucks promised.

But whilst Mavis was away, Toby arrived.
He decided to shunt the trucks himself.

The trucks decided to bump him anyway.
They reached the level crossing and Toby's
brakes came on.

This was the signal for the trucks.

"On, on, on," they yelled.

Toby was away, with the trucks screaming and yelling behind him.

No-one realised that melted snow had turned a stream into a torrent and the bridge above it was about to collapse.

The rails were now like a tightrope across
the thundering water.

"Stop! Stop!" cried Toby.

His driver fought for control. They came nearer and nearer to the bridge. The driver braked hard.

Toby stopped, still on the rails, but with his wheels treading the tightrope over the abyss.

Mavis was horrified and quickly came to the rescue.

Workmen anchored Toby with chains whilst she pulled the trucks away. Then she helped Toby to safety.

"I'm sorry about the trucks," said Mavis. "I can't think how you managed to stop them in time."

"Oh well," said Toby. "My driver told me about circus people who walk tightropes, but I just didn't fancy doing it myself."

Later the Fat Controller arrived.

"A *very* smart piece of work," he said. "Mavis, you did well too, I hear."

"It was my fault about those trucks Sir," she faltered. "But if I could…"

"Could what?"

"Come down the line sometimes Sir.
Toby says he'll show me what to do."

"Certainly," replied the Fat Controller.
"If your Manager agrees."

And so it was arranged.

Now Mavis is as happy as can be and the Fat Controller thinks she's Really Useful indeed.

MEET ALL THESE FRIENDS IN BUZZ BOOKS:

Thomas the Tank Engine
The Animals of Farthing Wood
Biker Mice from Mars
Winnie-the-Pooh
Fireman Sam
Rupert
Babar

First published in Great Britain 1992 by Buzz Books
an imprint of Reed Children's Books
Michelin House, 81 Fulham Road, London SW3 6RB
and Auckland, Melbourne, Singapore and Toronto
Reprinted 1993, 1994, 1995

ISBN 1 85591 225 2

Printed and bound in Italy by Olivotto